Pali and the Patchy Monster

Written and Illustrated by Katerina Tadenev

DEDICATED TO

Дедушка
Бабушка

Alex

All my friends

The family

My Mom

SHM

Max &
Reinhardt
(the cats)

The girl was always taking lefts on rights and ups on downs.
She was curious, inquisitive, and creative.

But mostly, she was a brat.

She called herself Pali the Destroyer.
Her parents called her Pali.
Mostly the did not call her anything.
They did not talk much.

One day Pali was walking down a dark, dreary, dangerous alley, as usual.

The alley was especially wet. Water ran down th pavement, greedily dragging garbage away fro and pooling over something shiny in the center

4

Pali tiptoed up to the shiny thing,
          crouched at the edge, and looked.
She looked until she knew that she had to
                    TAKE ACTION!
Or she wasn't PALI THE DESTROYER!

SPLAT!

She leapt right into the middle of the puddle.
Her footing was unstable as the shiny thing
wobble-tottered under her.

Pali looked down and saw that she
was standing on a manhole cover-
an unstable, shaky, adventurous cover.

"TAKE ME OUT!"

Demanded the manhole cover.

6

"I WOULD LOVE TO!"

Answered Pali, happily pulling
at the edge of the manhole.

She pulled and dragged and
dragged and pulled, eventually
pulling the cover right off!

"I dare you", said the cover admiring
her inquistiveness and creativity,

"TO DANCE ON THE EDGE"

"GLADLY!" Pali answered.
No one had told her not to
listen to manhole covers.

She jumped up and down,
Harder and harder,
Higher and higher,
She was getting really good at avoiding the hole,
and maintaining edginess.

But her shoes were not as great as her.

They had defects, setbacks, personality flaws,
personal issues... and worst of all,

SLIPPERY SOLES!

8

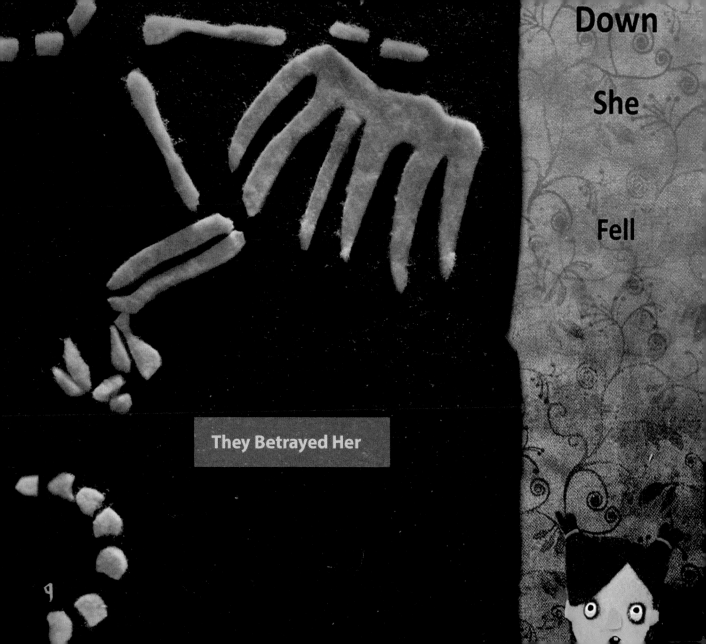

Pali tumbled out of the pipe.

...and came face to feet
        with Patchy Monster.

A unique monster who ate fabric pieces to keep up
the patchiness. A ferocious monster with giant teeth,
obligatory monster horns, and a fragile, soft filament
deep in his monster heart of hearts.

"Gwomp" said Patchy Monster, pointing to himself.

"Gwomp", "Gwomp."

The nickname "Gwomp" meant "Adorable Duckchild"
in his language but Pali was not aware of this,
  and did not care.

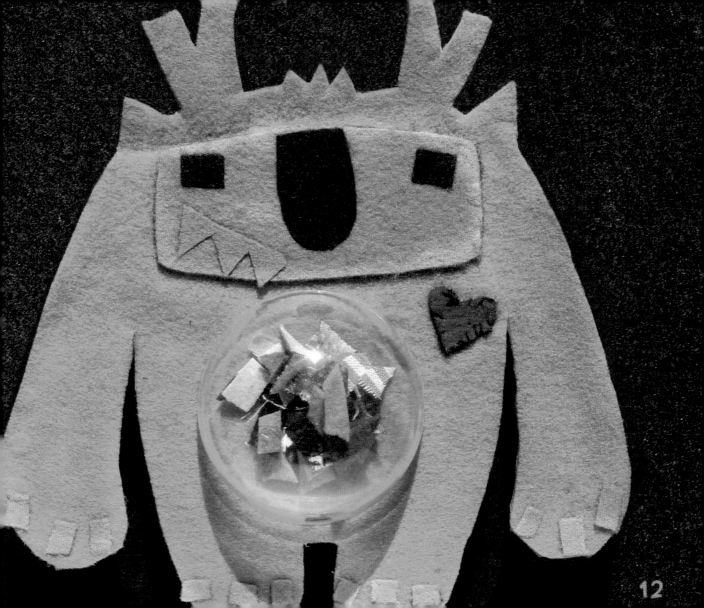

12

"Chomp!"
The girl bit the monster on his patchy slippers.

"CHOMP, CHOMP!"

"NOT NICE!"

Whimpered the monster indignantly.

"Those were brand new used slippers
from Monster Thrifts"

Patchy Monster leaned down to the small thing that hurt him.
A dull pain cascaded down his back and his eyes dimmed as
he leaned lower and lower. His hands searched around
his slippers, finally closing around the girl.

Pali rose up on a one-of-a-kind elevator made of paws.

Higher and higher.

Until she came to a crunching stop next to a toothy entrance.

Face to face with the monster.

16

The Patchy Monster swallowed the brat whole.

"I didn't pack my large PINK flippers with the deadly bunny pattern and other diving equipment!"
Screamed the girl.

But it was too late and no one heard her.

The Patchy Monster walked
heavily through Slimerion Town.

Down its sluggish slippery slopes
and up the slow snail spirals.

Sliding down the flat Foam Lands
on the other side of the town.

Where his tiny house was.
A small home for a big monster.

He made a turn into his walkway and
glumly sat down on a red boulder.

21

Usually the boulder made him happy,
he even kept a piece of yellow chalk
next to it to tally up happy feelings.

But today he did not pick up the chalk.

22

He looked into his transparent tummy.
Usually it was full of different colors, patterns,
and fabrics, but today the colorful
fish-bowl belly gave him no joy.

He could see the girl swirling around
and making nasty remarks about his weight
that he could not hear

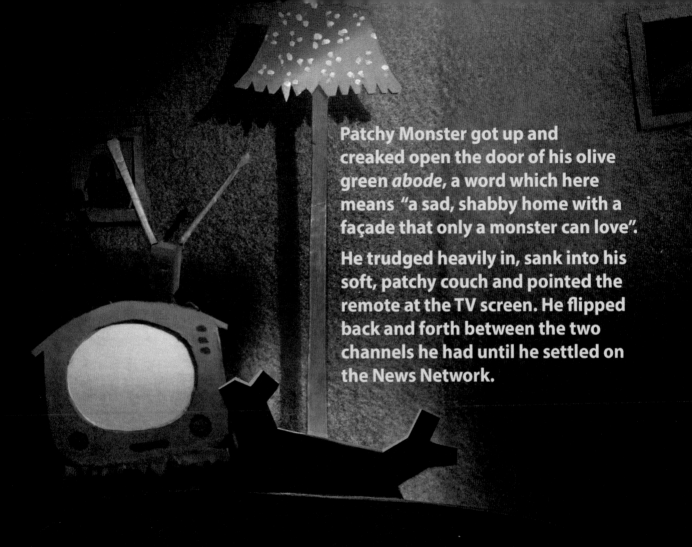

Patchy Monster got up and creaked open the door of his olive green *abode*, a word which here means "a sad, shabby home with a façade that only a monster can love".

He trudged heavily in, sank into his soft, patchy couch and pointed the remote at the TV screen. He flipped back and forth between the two channels he had until he settled on the News Network.

On the screen, two happy parents were declaring their deep feelings of sadness for a little missing girl. They twirled the loose ends of their fur coats and played with the little pink heart cufflinks on the ends of their coat sleeves. "She had better not lose her hat!" the mother declared angrily, and the father scowled.

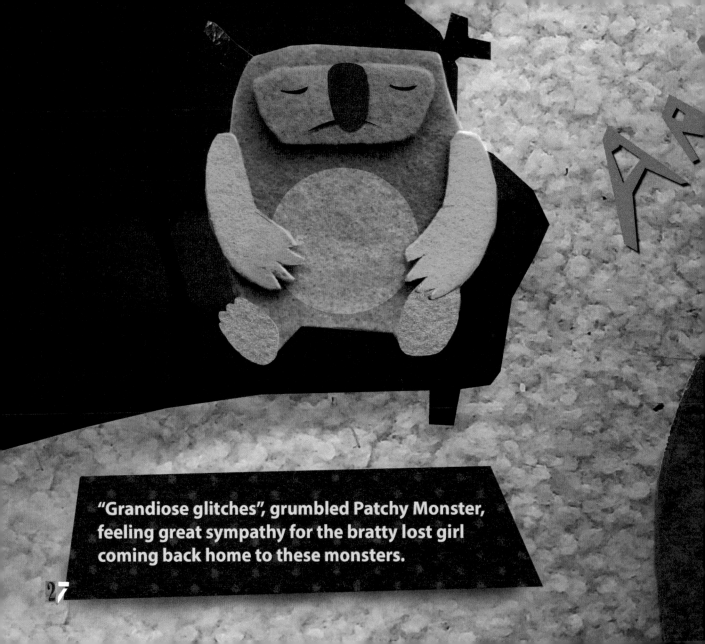

"Grandiose glitches", grumbled Patchy Monster, feeling great sympathy for the bratty lost girl coming back home to these monsters.

27

He glanced down into his transparent tummy.

The girl stared back at him.

And held up her fists.

The next morning Patchy knew what he had to do.

He had to think.

So he thought and thought and thought....

But...that did him no good, so he went to a doctor.

Dr. Snailtrails- the Monster's designated psychologist-
sat Patchy in a recliner and glared at him for half an hour.
He started by avoiding eye contact enitirely, then he barely
glanced at the the monster until Patchy felt intensely guilty.

And finally Dr. Snailtrails set his stalkly eyes in a straight
shot for Patchy Monster's and kept them set.

"WHAT IS WRONG WITH YOU? ",

he finally inquired.

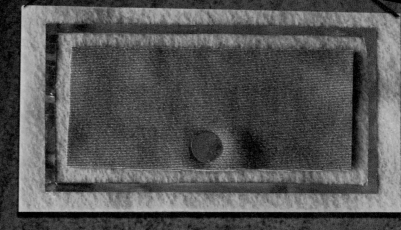

"I have swallowed a girl in purple overalls, and she..." Patchy began

"AN ANSWER IS UNNECESSARY!" Dr. Snailtrails interrupted.

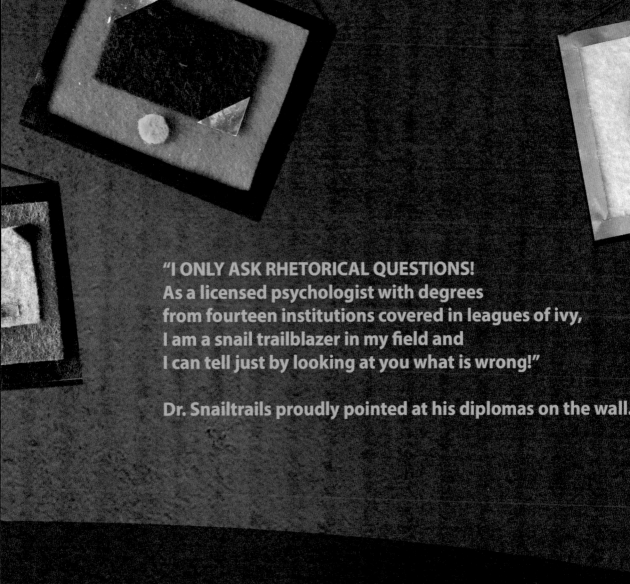

"I ONLY ASK RHETORICAL QUESTIONS!
As a licensed psychologist with degrees
from fourteen institutions covered in leagues of ivy,
I am a snail trailblazer in my field and
I can tell just by looking at you what is wrong!"

Dr. Snailtrails proudly pointed at his diplomas on the wall.

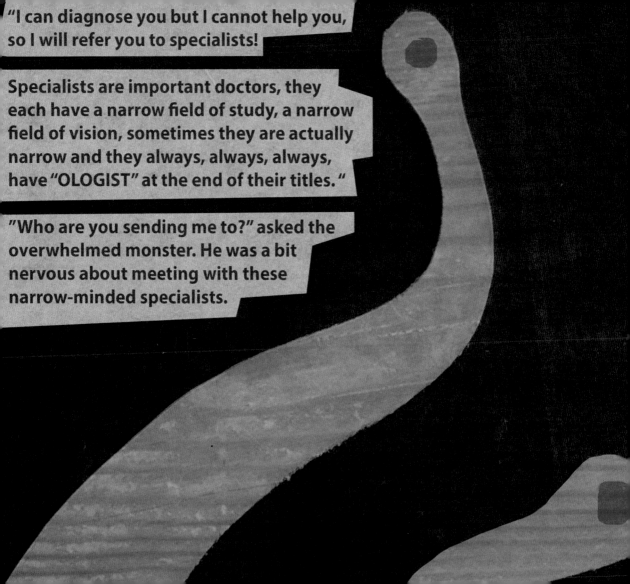

"I can diagnose you but I cannot help you, so I will refer you to specialists!

Specialists are important doctors, they each have a narrow field of study, a narrow field of vision, sometimes they are actually narrow and they always, always, always, have "OLOGIST" at the end of their titles. "

"Who are you sending me to?" asked the overwhelmed monster. He was a bit nervous about meeting with these narrow-minded specialists.

...eferring you", pronounced ...ailtrails, "to an ornithologist who studies ...ls that propel themselves in various ...ons in air by flapping their extremities."

"..." Patchy Monster muttered.

"..." the doctor bellowed, "then you will ...n astrologist who will tell you ...s in your stars!"

"...want to check my stomach," ... Patchy Monster tried to interject.

"...ce!" screamed Dr. Snailtrails, ...astly you will visit the Ear Doctor in ...ar Canals for good measure."

6

"Where are they all located?" asked the monster in defeat.

"The Ornithologist is down the hall on the left, the Astrologist is on the seventh hill from here in a tall tower and the Ear-Ologist is far, far away. You will probably find him at some point."

"Thanks..." said Patchy Monster and proceeded down the hall, grumbling about the healthcare system the whole way.

The Ornithologist was a stork in a stark white gown.
He did not talk much, but he made a lot of gestures to
compensate for the silence.

He started the procedure by gesturing at Patchy Monster's
stomach, flapping his wings, tapping his talons and poking
Patchy's transparent bubble with his long orange beak.

The latch did not open, and nothing significant happened.

40

Pali turned away from everyone in disgust and began to brood in boredom. As an "almost teenager", she had to practice that skill daily and was getting really good at it, but the stork abruptly stopped paying attention to her, and she immediately felt slighted and deeply offended on a personal level.

The stork wrote an indecipherable doctor's note on a soft piece of paper towel, signing the prescription by stomping on it with his clawed bird feet until it was in tatters and finally throwing it into the wastebasket.

"I can't help you" the doctor droned, unhappy that he had to make verbal communication.

"The problem is out of my Area of Expertise, try next town over."

So the Patchy Monster left the stork's Area of Expertise. He walked slowly across the seven hills in search of the Astrologist. Meanwhile Pali was lying on the pile of fabric pieces at the bottom of Patchy's stomach. She was trying to fall asleep to the rhythm of the monster's big steps.

Crash
Crash

−1

Crunch
It was hard to sleep no matter how many sheep she added and subtracted.

Crash, crash, crunch,

Crunch...

Crunch

+1

Crunch

+2

44

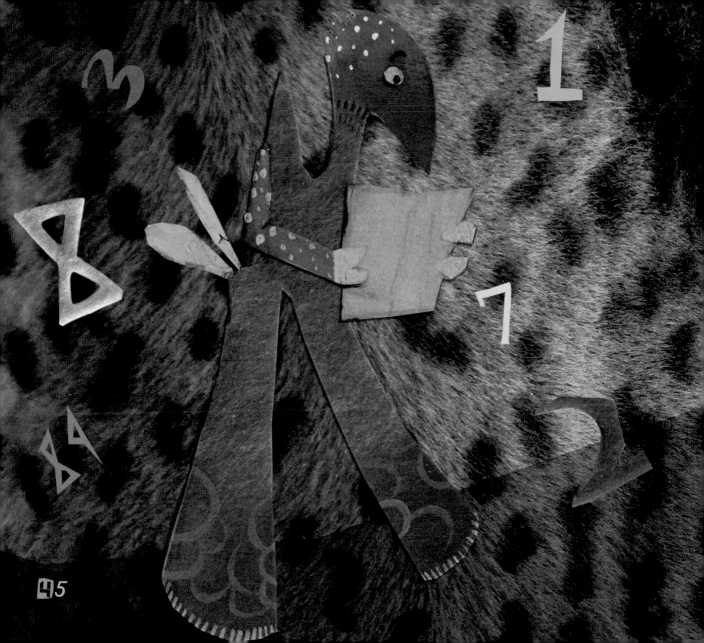

The astrologist counted everything and made everything count.

He counted the 38 floors inside his tall, lukewarm, leopard-print house and the 38 billion stars outside of it. He made his pet frog count the toes on his seven-toed cat and he made the cat count the crickets that his pet frog dined on. The astrologist greeted everybody with a clipboard because he thought it made him look more important.

"Bonjour" said the Astrologist in French
as he flung the door open. He greeted
visitors in French to sound more important.
"Nice to meet you", answered Patchy.
It was not nice to meet the Astrologist
but Patchy was a polite monster.

"How can an important, clip-boarded
man with a glamorous seven-toed cat,
help you?" asked the Astrologist haughtily.

"My psychologist send me here, so I hope
that you can open the latch on my stomach
and release the girl who is trapped inside."

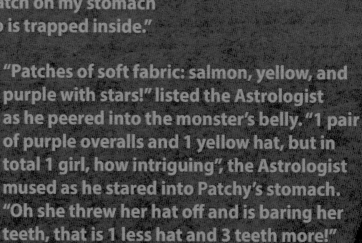

"Patches of soft fabric: salmon, yellow, and
purple with stars!" listed the Astrologist
as he peered into the monster's belly. "1 pair
of purple overalls and 1 yellow hat, but in
total 1 girl, how intriguing", the Astrologist
mused as he stared into Patchy's stomach.
"Oh she threw her hat off and is baring her
teeth, that is 1 less hat and 3 teeth more!"

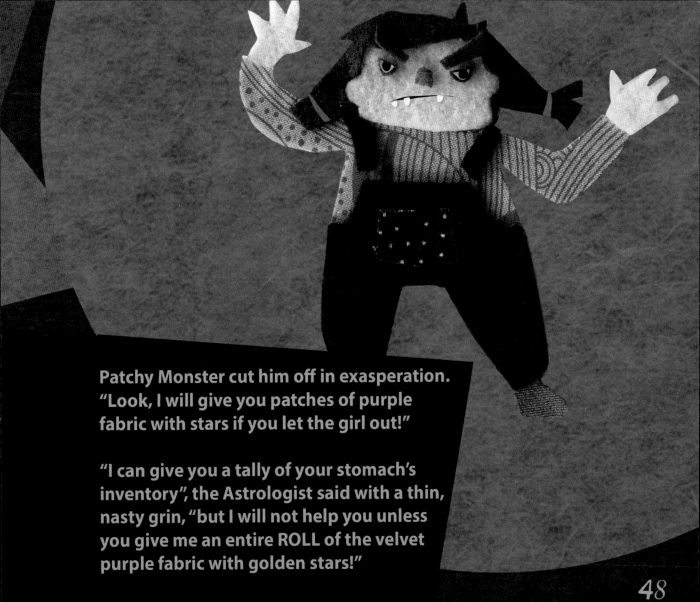

Patchy Monster cut him off in exasperation. "Look, I will give you patches of purple fabric with stars if you let the girl out!"

"I can give you a tally of your stomach's inventory", the Astrologist said with a thin, nasty grin, "but I will not help you unless you give me an entire ROLL of the velvet purple fabric with golden stars!"

It was definitely not very nice to meet the Astrologist and without another word Patchy Monster and Pali walked off the property to search for the Ear Doctor.

The sun slowly sank down and Patchy became more downtrodden as he trod down the hills.

He rumbled as the girl tumbled inside.

49

50

Before the last ray of sunlight hid under the valley, Patchy found a grove of trees to pass the night in. He pushed together leaves and rested on the crunchy pile, closing his eyes.

"Knock,"

"Knock,"

"Knock."

He looked at Pali and she smiled at him, waving goodnight. As the first star peeked out in the night sky the little girl picked up a piece of velvet fabric and wrapped herself tightly in it.

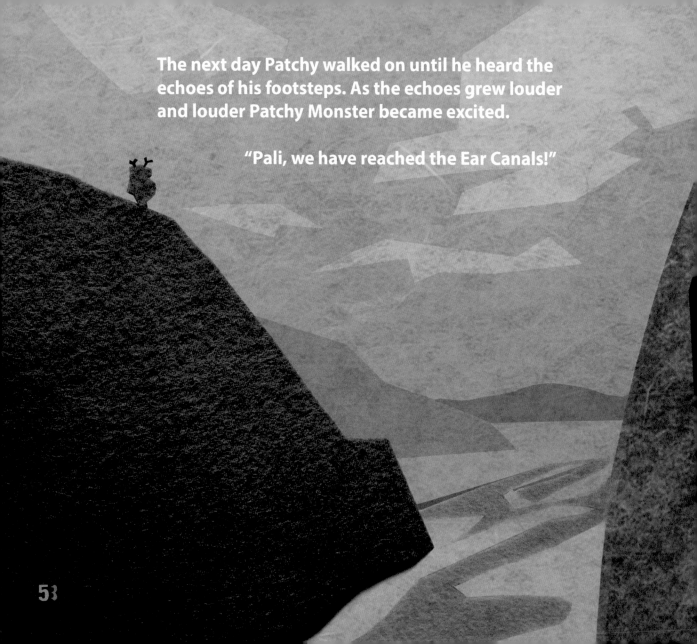

The next day Patchy walked on until he heard the echoes of his footsteps. As the echoes grew louder and louder Patchy Monster became excited.

"Pali, we have reached the Ear Canals!"

The monster huffed and puffed as he squeezed through the dried-out riverbed, and the tall hills around him huffed and puffed back.

The echoes told him to turn many rights
                until he circled into a corner.

    and out of the corner of the Giant Ear,

                        the Monster heard...

SILENCE.

Deafening, piercing, all-surrounding silence.
Patchy listened and listened but nothing happened.

Dejectedly the monster slumped into the corner in despair.
"There is no one to help us Pali" he whispered sadly.
"I do not think that the doctor will come."

Tap,

tap, tap,

tap, tap, tap,

Pali was trying to reach out to the monster from the inside of his belly. She had something in her hand and was tapping with it against the transparent wall.

"I am sorry" Patchy Monster cried,
   "I cannot help you!
         I AM SO SORRY!"

Creak,
      creak,

         creak!

Something inside of the Monster was moving!

Could it be the door on his tummy?

Patchy stared down in surprise as the girl- the curious, creative, bratty girl in purple overalls and a yellow hat- cracked the latch open and leapt out of his stomach.

They stared at one another.

Pali victoriously held out a needle.

"I found this and poked at the lock!"

"I made you something!"
    exclaimed the girl and dashed back into his stomach.

A long cape followed her as she climbed back out.

"I found this needle and used the strings in my yellow hat to sew you a giant blanket made up of all the pieces inside of you!"

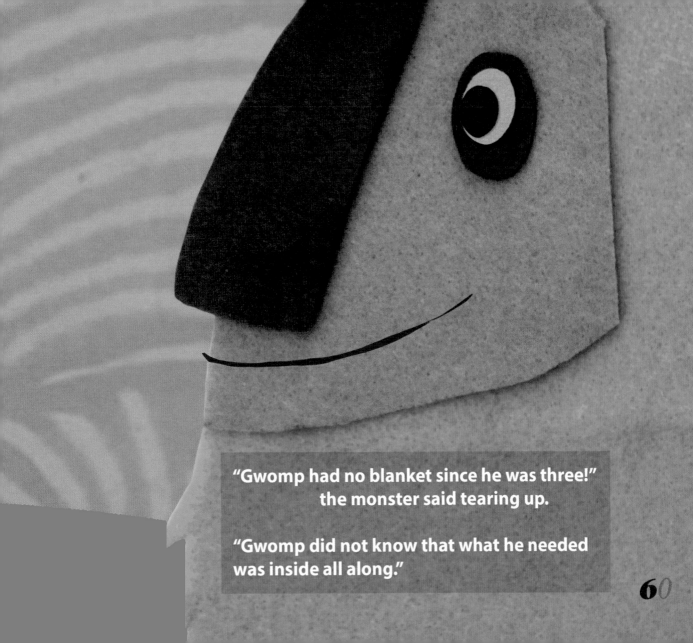

"Gwomp had no blanket since he was three!"
the monster said tearing up.

"Gwomp did not know that what he needed
was inside all along."

60

Pali grinned and grabbed the Monster's hand.

They stopped searching for the Ear Doctor, they called him a few times but he was out of earshot so they left.

They did not need "ologists" anymore, they had each other and went on many more adventures every time that Pali visited the Underground.

Made in the USA
Monee, IL
04 December 2019